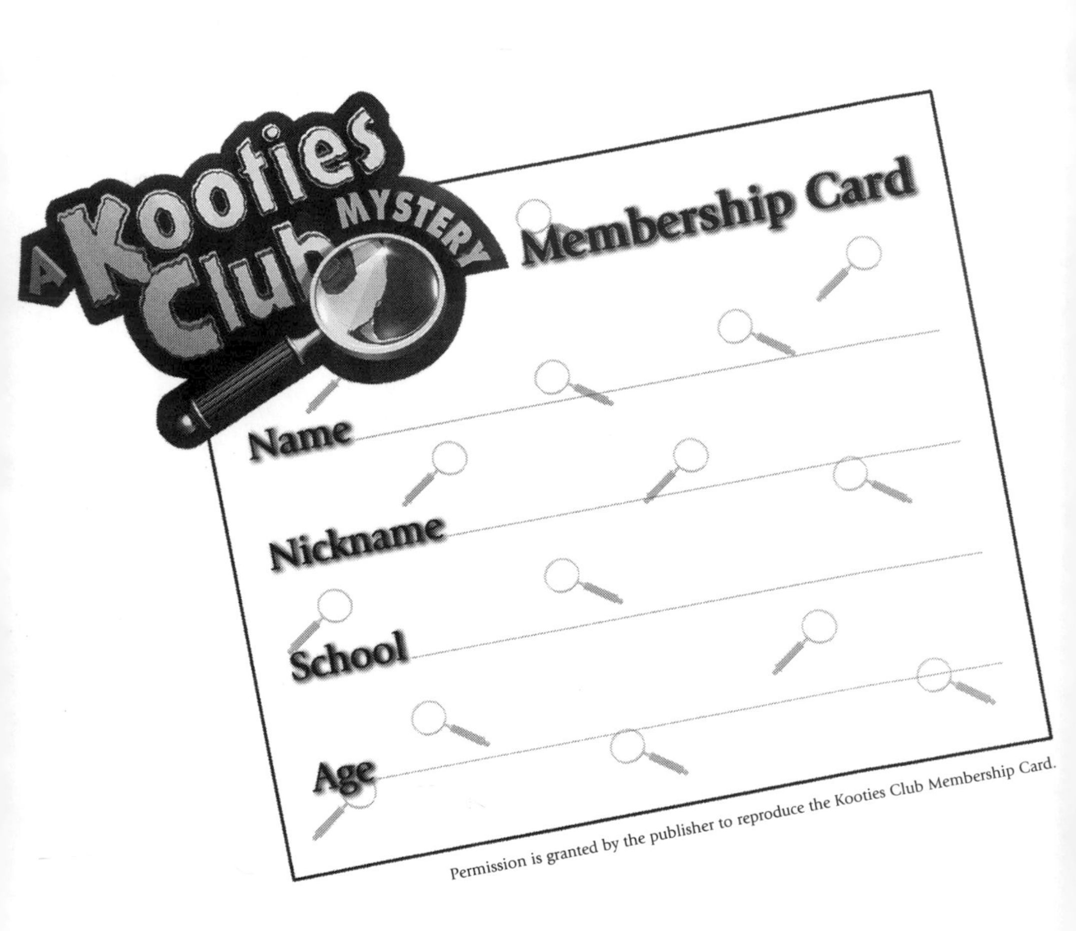
A Kooties Club MYSTERY
Membership Card
Name
Nickname
School
Age

# The Mystery of the Big Paw Print

by M. J. Cosson

Perfection Learning® CA

Cover and Inside Illustrations: Michael A. Aspengren


Printed in the United States of America.

For information, contact
Perfection Learning® Corporation,
1000 North Second Avenue, P.O. Box 500,
Logan, Iowa 51546-1099.
Paperback 0-7891-2297-9
Cover Craft® 0-7807-7267-9
8 9 10 PP 09 08 07 06

# Table of Contents

Introduction . . . . . . . . . . . . . . . . . 6

Chapter 1. The Sighting . . . . . . . . . . 10

Chapter 2. The Proof Is in the Print . . . . 16

Chapter 3. The Stakeout . . . . . . . . . 21

Chapter 4. The Plan . . . . . . . . . . . . 27

Chapter 5. The Plan in Action . . . . . . . . 31

Chapter 6. The Best-Laid Plans . . . . . . . 35

Chapter 7. What Now? . . . . . . . . . . 38

Chapter 8. Will Anything Work? . . . . . . . 43

Chapter 9. Al Jackson . . . . . . . . . . 47

Chapter 10. The Beast . . . . . . . . . . . 51

# Introduction

Abe, Ben, Gabe, Toby, and Ty live in a large city. There isn't much for kids to do. There isn't even a park close by.

Their neighborhood is made up of apartment houses and trailer parks. Gas stations and small shops stand where the parks and grass used to be. And there aren't many houses with big yards.

Ty and Abe live in an apartment complex. Next door is a large vacant lot. It is full of brush, weeds, and trash. A path runs across the lot. On the other side is a trailer park. Ben and Toby live there.

Across the street from the trailer park is a big gray house. Gabe lives in the top apartment of the house.

The five boys have known each other since they started school. But they haven't always been friends.

The other kids say the boys have cooties. And the other kids won't touch them with a ten-foot pole. So Abe, Ben, Gabe, Toby, and Ty have formed their own club. They call it the Kooties Club.

Here's how to join. If no one else will have anything to do with you, you're in.

The boys call themselves the Koots for short. Ben's grandma calls his grandpa an *old coot.* And Ben thinks his grandpa is pretty cool. So if he's an old coot, Ben and his friends must be young koots.

The Koots play ball and hang out with each other. But most of all, they look for mysteries to solve.

*Chapter 1*

# The Sighting

The sky opened up. Rain poured from every cloud. White flashes lit the night. A loud boom cracked through the quiet.

Abe couldn't sleep with all the flashes and noise. He looked out his bedroom window. He lived in a ground-floor apartment. His window faced the parking lot.

Suddenly, a man rushed by. Something huge followed the man. It

was too fast for Abe to tell what it was. It looked too big to be a dog.

But it did have four legs. Was it chasing the man? Was the man in danger?

Another white flash lit the sky. Another loud boom sounded. Abe shut the drapes. He lay back on his pillow. "What was that?" he wondered. "I've never seen anything so big!"

The next morning, the sun shone brightly. It was time to head for school.

The Koots met in the parking lot. On the way to school, they joked and laughed. They talked about what had happened since yesterday.

Abe told the Koots what he had seen.

"Just a dream," said Ty.

"Just a dog," added Ben.

"Just your eyes playing tricks," laughed Toby.

"But maybe you did see something," said Gabe. He looked at Abe curiously. "What do you think it was?"

"I don't know," replied Abe. His voice shook a little as he spoke. "Maybe it was a tiger," he added softly.

"Tigers don't live here," said Ty.

"Maybe it got out of the zoo. Or maybe it's really a mountain lion. It could have come down from the mountains," said Gabe excitedly. "Maybe we should check it out."

"Okay," said Toby. He was always ready for a mystery. "Let's meet after school. Try to think of ways we can find out what Abe saw."

After school, the Koots met by the big tree in front of the school. "Let's go to my house," suggested Gabe. "We can sit on my roof and look for the tiger. Or whatever Abe saw."

The boys rushed into the house where Gabe lived. They ran upstairs to his apartment and threw open the front door. Without stopping, they hurried to Gabe's room.

Gabe opened his window. And the boys climbed onto the porch roof. It was hard to see very far. There were too many trees around the house.

"A tiger could be in one of these trees," said Abe. "It could climb down at night and eat people. It could jump onto this roof."

"Sure, whatever," said Ty, rolling his eyes. "I told you we don't have tigers here. Anyway, don't you think someone would see it? I still think you were dreaming."

Abe looked away. He felt hurt. "I know that I saw something last night," he said. "And I will prove it to you!"

Abe had had enough. He thought, "If they don't believe me, that's fine! I saw something. And I'm going to find out what it was. With or without them!"

Abe climbed back through the window, leaving the other boys on the roof. He was going home.

He ran through the vacant lot. The trees were scary. After he passed the trees, he slowed down. He walked along with his head down.

All of a sudden, Abe stopped. His mouth flew open in surprise. He ran back to Gabe's house.

"Come quick," he yelled. "I found proof!"

*Chapter 2*

# The Proof Is in the Print

The Koots followed Abe. He led them across the empty lot. "Look," he said. He pointed to the ground. There was a big paw print in the mud.

"Wow!" shouted Ben. "This print is too big to be from a dog!"

Abe held his hand over the print. It was bigger than Abe's hand.

Whatever made the print was huge! It must be gigantic!

The other Koots squatted. They studied the print. It was the biggest paw print they had ever seen.

"OK, Abe. Now I believe you," said Ty, looking up at Abe.

"Me too," added the rest of the guys. Abe grinned.

The Koots turned to walk back to Gabe's house. They looked up into the trees. "Let's get out of here!" one of them yelled. They tore across the lot without looking back.

Finally, they were safe inside the apartment. Gabe turned on the news. No big animal had escaped from the zoo. There wasn't anyone killed by a big animal. In fact, no one had reported seeing a large animal.

"This animal could be dangerous. What are we going to do?" asked Ben.

"Call 911," answered Abe.

"But we haven't really seen it," said Ty. "We need proof."

"I know!" shouted Toby. "We need to show the paw print to someone. We can copy it and take it to the police!"

"And just how do you make a copy of a paw print?" asked Ben.

"You get some stuff. Then you mix it up," Toby explained.

He continued, "Then you pour it into the print. When it gets hard, you take it out. It makes a copy of the print. Then you take it to the police," Toby explained.

"Okay," said Ty. "Let's do it. What do we use?"

"I don't know," answered Gabe. "Let's go look at the print again."

"What about the tiger?" asked Abe.

"Maybe the animal only comes out at night. And it's daytime. So we'll be okay," reasoned Ty. "And there's safety in numbers. There are five of us and only one of it. So if it gets one of us, the other four can run for help!"

"Great," said Ben.

The boys walked back to where they had found the paw print. The sun had dried the ground. Gabe brought an old bowl. He picked up a stick. The others found a mud puddle. They mixed up some new mud in the bowl. Then they poured it into the print.

The Koots waited for the new mud to dry. They took turns blowing on the mud and watching for the tiger. It seemed to take a long time for the new mud to dry.

The boys looked at the sky. It was getting dark. It was time for big animals to come out. That meant it was time for the boys to finish and get inside.

At last, the new mud was dry. But when Gabe and Ty tried to pick it up, it stuck to the paw print. Everything was a mess. But worst of all, the print was gone!

The Koots looked at each other. Where would they get proof now? They split up and went home.

Later in his bed, Abe watched and waited for the big animal. Suddenly it streaked past his window just before he fell asleep.

*Chapter 3*

# The Stakeout

The next morning, Abe begged his mom to let the Koots sleep over. After all, it was Friday. There was no school the next day. At last, she agreed. Kim, Abe's sister, would sleep with Grandma.

After supper, the Koots came over. They brought blankets, bedrolls, and sleeping bags. They promised Abe's mom and dad that they would keep the noise down.

It was raining again. The rain rolled down Abe's window in sheets. The Koots sat at the window and watched. It seemed like forever. They didn't see a tiger or any other big animal.

"Maybe it's too wet," Abe finally said.

"When you saw it the first time, it was raining," Gabe reminded him.

"Maybe it's full tonight," offered Toby. "Maybe it ate something big. And now it's sleeping."

"Yeah, maybe it ate a dog. Or a little kid," Ty laughed.

"Very funny. Maybe it did eat Al Jackson's little dog, Lucky," said Abe.

"Now that I think of it, when was the last time you saw Lucky?" Ty asked.

"Not for a while," answered Abe. They looked at each other.

"Anybody want to play cards?" asked Gabe. He took out a deck and began to shuffle them.

The Koots played cards. They took turns watching out the window. Soon, the boys were asleep. All but Abe and Toby. They sat on Abe's bed watching the rain.

Toby stretched and yawned. He looked back out the window just as a big animal ran past.

Abe and Toby looked at each other in shock. They looked at the clock. It was 2 a.m. It had stopped raining.

On Saturday morning, Toby told the others that he had seen the big animal too.

"What was it?" asked Ben.

"I don't think it was a tiger," answered Toby. "It was too tall to be some kind of cat. It was really big. I don't know what it could be. I know one thing. I wouldn't want to meet it in a dark alley."

"Maybe it's Bigfoot!" said Gabe.

"Maybe it is," agreed Abe. "That would explain why it's so huge. He

probably hides somewhere on the vacant lot."

Abe grinned. He was so glad someone else had seen the beast.

"Hey, Abe," Ty said. "Remember Lucky? Let's ask Al if we can take him for a walk. Then we'll know he's okay."

The boys hurried into the kitchen. Abe's mom made the boys sit down for breakfast. Juice, milk, and sweet rolls sat on the table. The boys tried not to hurry. But they had important business to take care of. They thanked Abe's mom and dad and rushed out the door.

The Koots went to Al Jackson's apartment to ask if they could walk Lucky. Al was always glad to let the kids walk his dog. Then he didn't have to do it.

Ty rang the doorbell. After a minute, a voice came from inside. "Who's there?"

"It's Ty and some friends."

"What do you want?" asked the voice gruffly.

"Can we walk Lucky?" Ty yelled.

"He's gone," answered the voice.

"Where is he?" hollered Ty.

"Just gone. Now go away and leave me alone!" said the voice.

"Not a good sign," whispered Ben as they walked away.

*Chapter 4*

# The Plan

"Now what do we do?" asked Abe.

"Let's go to my house," suggested Toby. "We need to make a plan. And I have to find out something."

The Koots walked carefully across the empty lot. They kept an eye out for signs of Bigfoot. They didn't find any new paw prints in the mud.

Toby stopped at the trailer next door to his. He rang the doorbell. A lady came to the door.

"Hi, Mrs. Wells," said Toby. "Have you seen Tom lately?"

"Hi, Toby," Mrs. Wells said. "No, I haven't seen Tom Cat for two or three days now. He must have run off again."

Toby looked at the Koots. They all nodded to each other.

"Okay, thanks, Mrs. Wells," Toby said with a smile. His look said it all.

The boys went inside Toby's trailer. They shut the door to his room. "Okay," Toby said. "This is bad news. Two animals have disappeared. We have to do something soon. Or somebody's going to get hurt."

"I have an idea," Gabe offered. "We can build a trap."

"And just how do you build a trap for such a big animal?" asked Ben. "I hope this idea is better than making a copy of the paw print."

"I saw it in a movie," Gabe explained. "You dig a hole and cover it with brush. When the animal runs down the path, it falls in. Then you have to get someone with a big net to get it out."

"So, Mr. Smart Guy, who do we call to get it out?" asked Ty.

"The zoo," explained Gabe. "We call the zoo!"

"Okay, let's do it," said Ty. "Who has a shovel?"

"I don't," answered Abe.

"I don't," answered Ben.

"Me neither," added Toby.

"Well, it's lucky that I do," said Gabe. "We can take turns digging."

The Koots ran to Gabe's house and got the shovel. They found a snow shovel too.

"We can use this to lift the dirt out of the hole," said Gabe. "Let's go!" He had now taken charge.

*Chapter 5*

# The Plan in Action

Gabe led the others to the place where Abe had found the paw print.

"Let's dig here." Gabe pointed to a spot. "I'll start."

The boys dug for two hours. By noon, they had a hole one foot deep.

"This will take all afternoon!" cried Toby. "I'd better go eat lunch. One of you other guys go too. The rest of you keep digging. When we get back, the others can go to lunch. Then we'll dig."

By late afternoon, the boys had a hole that was four feet deep. The dirt at the bottom was as hard as rock. They were too tired to dig anymore.

Gabe sighed. "I don't think we can ever make this deep enough."

"I know," agreed Toby. "If Bigfoot falls in this, it will just get mad. Then someone will really get hurt!"

"And we've left our scent. So it will come after us," Abe added. "I wish we hadn't started this hole."

Ty held up the shovel. "Well, are we going to quit or are we going to finish this?" he asked. "If we do the best we can, the animal may at least break a leg."

"Okay," said Gabe. "Keep digging, Ty. I'll get some leaves and sticks to cover the hole."

The other Koots helped Gabe. They found dead branches and limbs. They heaped their findings beside the hole. All the time, Ty kept digging.

The boys built up the dirt around the edge of the hole. Now the hole was almost six feet deep!

Ty had a hard time climbing out. The other Koots pulled him out with the shovel.

The Koots placed the big limbs over the hole. Then they piled on branches and sticks. Last, they covered everything with leaves.

Ben looked at the trap. "If I didn't know there was a hole under there, I would walk right over it," he said. The other Koots agreed. It did look like a pretty good trap!

"Let's meet back here in the morning. We should catch something by then," said Gabe. "We'll meet at eight sharp."

The Koots gave the Kootie handshake and then headed home.

Later, Abe was too tired to keep his eyes open. He was asleep when the beast ran past his window.

*Chapter 6*

# The Best-Laid Plans

On Sunday morning, Abe was having a hard time waking up. All of a sudden, he remembered the trap. He jumped out of bed and pulled on his pants. He pulled a shirt over his head and stepped into his shoes.

The clock said 7:59. Ty was at the door waiting for him. They ran over to the lot.

Ben, Toby, and Gabe were already there. A look of horror was on each of their faces.

As Abe and Ty got closer, they heard someone yelling. That someone was one of their neighbors. She looked very mad. She was shaking her finger at the other Koots.

"This path is used by joggers all the time," she yelled. "You could have killed me! I almost fell in there. I could have broken my neck!"

Suddenly, she saw Ty and Abe. She turned to them. "Are you the other boys who almost killed me? I was jogging, and I almost fell into this hole. Who are your parents? I am going to call every one of them."

"You will fill this hole in today!" the lady continued. "Right now! And I hope your parents ground you for at least a week!"

The lady reached into the small pack she carried around her waist. She pulled out a small notepad and a pencil. Each boy gave his name and phone number.

As she left, she yelled, "I will be back in one hour. That hole had better be gone!"

Gabe looked at Toby. Toby looked at Ty. Ty looked at Abe. Abe looked at Ben. Ben looked at Gabe. "I guess we'd better start digging," they all said at once. Gabe ran to get the shovels.

*Chapter 7*

# What Now?

That afternoon, every Koot sat on his own bed. They were grounded. Each had been told to think about what a dumb idea it was to dig a trap where people walk. But each boy was thinking about something else. How were they going to catch the big animal?

Ty thought he'd watch for Al Jackson. If just one kid talked to him, maybe Al would say what happened to Lucky. That was Ty's plan.

Toby thought about how many cats and dogs were missing. He planned to go to every trailer that had a pet. He would ask about the pets. If a lot of pets were missing, Toby would call the police. That was Toby's plan.

Ben made a list.

1. Call the zoo. Ask if any big animal had escaped.

2. Call the park ranger. Ask if there were any reports of wild animals on the loose.
3. Call the newspaper. Tell them there may be a big story.

That was Ben's plan.

Gabe left his bed and sat out on the roof. He would climb up on the top of the house. From there, he would be able to see the whole neighborhood. Just maybe he would spot the beast. That was Gabe's plan.

Abe looked out his window. He told his parents there was a tiger in the neighborhood. They didn't believe him. Now he had to prove there was. Abe thought about using a camera. His grandma had a camera. He would take a picture that night. That was Abe's plan.

All Sunday afternoon, the Koots sat and thought. At last, their moms let them out of their rooms. They went to work.

*Chapter 8*

# Will Anything Work?

"Grandma, can I use your camera?" Abe asked.

"What for?" asked Grandma.

"I need to take a picture to prove there is a tiger. But I can't take the picture until very late," answered Abe.

"I'm sorry, honey. My flash isn't working. You won't get anything," replied Grandma.

So much for Abe's plan.

Toby went to every trailer in the park. He found that Tom was the only cat missing. And no dogs were missing. Toby didn't know what to think. So much for Toby's plan.

Gabe's mom came into his room to check on him. He wasn't there. He was way up on the roof. Gabe returned to his room and was told that he couldn't go out all week. So much for Gabe's plan.

Ben called the zoo. No big animals were missing. He called the park ranger. There weren't any reports about wild animals on the loose. Ben didn't know if he should call the newspaper. Maybe there wasn't a big story after all. So much for Ben's plan.

Ty walked over to Al Jackson's apartment. He stood outside. He listened for Lucky. He heard a long, low growl. But nothing else. And the growl certainly wasn't from Lucky!

Ty looked for Al Jackson's car. It wasn't in the parking lot. Ty went to get his yo-yo. He would wait for Al to come back.

Ty waited until after dark. Al didn't come back, and Ty had to go inside. So much for Ty's plan.

*Chapter 9*

# Al Jackson

On Monday morning, the Koots walked to school together. Toby, Ben, Abe, and Gabe told what they had done Sunday afternoon. No one had much to report.

Ty didn't say anything. They all looked at him. He was hiding something.

"What's up, Ty?" asked Gabe. "Did you find out anything?"

"Not for sure," said Ty. "But I think Al Jackson knows something."

Ty continued, "Let me check on it tonight. I'll let you know if I find anything."

"Can I come?" asked Abe. "You shouldn't be alone. What if something happens? You might need some help."

"Okay," answered Ty. "But you have to do just what I say."

Ty and Abe agreed to call the others and tell them what happened.

After school, Ty and Abe kicked a soccer ball in the parking lot. They could see Al Jackson's apartment. They waited for Al to come home

from work. At last, Al drove his car into the lot.

"Hey, Al," Ty and Abe yelled.

"Hey, guys," said Al. He got out of his car. Ty and Abe followed Al to his apartment. He opened the door a crack. As he started in, Ty stopped him.

"Can we come in?" asked Ty.

"No," answered Al.

"Well, we just wanted to tell you how sorry we are about Lucky," said Ty.

"Thanks, guys," said Al. He quickly entered the apartment and shut the door. Ty and Abe stood there staring at each other.

"So, what's going on?" asked Abe.

"I think there's something fishy in Al's apartment," answered Ty.

"What do you mean? Do you think he has Lucky tied up in there?" Abe asked.

"No," said Ty. "But I think he has something in there. I heard a noise. I don't know what it was. But it sure wasn't Lucky."

"Let's spy on Al," said Abe.

Ty and Abe spent the rest of the day watching Al's apartment. Al didn't come out. No one went in. At last, the boys had to go home.

That night, no one went running by Abe's window. And no big animal ran by. But Abe wasn't there to notice.

*Chapter 10*

# The Beast

It was very dark. There was no moon, and the parking lot light was burned out.

Abe and Ty hid by a bush. They were close to Al's apartment. It was after ten at night.

Abe and Ty had left their apartments without anyone seeing them. They were spying on Al Jackson.

An hour went by, and Al didn't come out. Abe and Ty were getting tired.

At last, Al opened the door slightly. He stuck his head out and looked all around. It was hard to see him in the shadows.

"What's he looking for?" whispered Abe.

"Shhh!" replied Ty.

Al stepped out of his apartment. He started running. Something huge ran out with him. It was as big as he was!

Ty and Abe jumped as it ran right by them. It stopped. It knew they were there! It made the same long, low growl that Ty had heard earlier.

Al kept running. The big animal came close to the bush. The boys closed their eyes and held their breath. Suddenly, it turned and ran after Al.

That was a close one! Ty and Abe looked at each other. The animal missed them. But the mystery was solved!

When Al came back, Ty and Abe were waiting by his door.

"What are you guys still doing up?" asked Al.

"We wanted to meet your new dog," said Ty.

"Okay, guys," said Al. "You got me." The huge dog stood behind him. It was almost as tall as he was.

Al explained, "This is Ajax. He is a Great Dane. My friend Linda has

Lucky. We traded dogs. Ajax was too much dog for her. Since we can't have big dogs here, I've been hiding Ajax. I'm moving to a house tomorrow. It's in the country. Ajax will have more room there. He can run all he wants."

Ty and Abe looked at Ajax's paws. His big paws would certainly make very big paw prints, especially in soft mud! They grinned.

"We have to get inside," said Al. "I have to hide Ajax. Later, guys."

"Bye, Al. Say bye to Lucky for us."

The boys turned to head home. Abe stopped and frowned.

"Do you have a key to your apartment?" he asked.

"No," said Ty. He frowned and looked at Abe. "Do you?"

"No," answered Abe. "I guess we'll have to ring our doorbells."

"My mom will be mad!" said Ty.

"Mine too," said Abe. "Oh well, at least we solved the mystery. Case closed."

They gave the Kootie handshake and headed home.